The
Littles
and the Lost Children

by **John Peterson**
Pictures by **Roberta Carter Clark**
Cover illustration by **Jacqueline Rogers**

A
LITTLE APPLE
PAPERBACK

SCHOLASTIC INC.
New York   Toronto   London   Auckland   Sydney

ISBN 0-590-43026-2

22 21 20   9/9 0 1/0

Printed in the U.S.A.   40

First Scholastic printing, January 1991

To Mark Ole and Kristin Lily

"Uncle Nick—it's your turn to tell a story," said Lucy Little, aged eight. "Tell us the story about the Small-Frys again. I love it."

"No, Lucy," said Uncle Nick. "I've told that story for the last time."

"Aw!" said Lucy's ten-year-old brother, Tom. "Come on, Uncle Nick. Please!"

Uncle Nick held a book up for everyone to see. "I won't *tell* the story, because I'm going to *read* it!" said Uncle Nick. He smiled. "Yes, sir, I've written my first book. I'm an author now. A small book for tiny people."

The Littles were indeed tiny people. The tallest Little—Tom's and Lucy's father, Mr. William T. Little—was only six inches tall. The tiny Littles lived in a small ten-room apartment inside the walls of a house owned by Mr. George Bigg. Mr. Bigg was a regular-sized person. He and his wife and their son,

Henry, never knew the Littles were living in the same house with them. The Littles were careful not to show themselves when the Biggs were around.

Even though they were tiny, the Littles looked like ordinary people. The one difference was—the Littles had tails! The tails weren't useful. They just looked good, the Littles thought.

Because the Littles stayed hidden from the Biggs a lot, they had to find ways to entertain themselves in their apartment. A favorite thing was to read or tell stories. This evening everyone turned to Uncle Nick and his new book.

"Read your story to us, Uncle Nick," said Mrs. Little. She cradled her seven-month-old baby in her arms. "I don't think Baby Betsy has heard it."

"Mother!" said Lucy. "Babies can't understand stories."

"Don't be so sure of that," said Mr. Little.

"Babies are smarter than you think, Lucy," said Cousin Dinky Little.

"Say no more!" commanded Uncle Nick, "or you might give away the most important part. Just settle back and listen. It's a remarkable tale, and it really happened."

The Small-Frys were a tiny family. They lived in a mudhouse near the top of Smoke Mountain. The Small-Frys and their neighbors—ten other Hill Tiny families—lived in a village of mudhouses. All the houses faced south to catch the sun's rays coming from the southern sky.

The Hill Tinies lived in the woods among the animals. They were friendly with many of them, and some animals even worked for the tiny people. But other animals were dangerous, especially the meat-eating animals. A two-inch-long shrew could, and would if it had the chance, make a meal out of a Hill Tiny.

In the village of mudhouses, everyone had a craft. One family made furniture. Another made pottery of all kinds. Others farmed and provided food for the village. Some made clothes. Instead of going to stores as big people did, the Hill Tinies traded with each other. In that way everybody got what they needed without making everything themselves.

The craft the Small-Frys worked at was the making of fabrics. They made cloth, felt, lace—and because Mother Lyn Small and Father Len Fry (the Small-Frys) were artists, their fabrics were as beautiful as they were well made.

It was Father Len's job to find the leaves, berries, and roots from which to make the colored dyes. And he gathered other materials that were needed to spin the thread for the cloth.

Mother Lyn did most of the weaving in the workshop at the back of the mudhouse. The Small-Frys' house was halfway up a steep part of Smoke Mountain. The rear of the house was dug into the side of the hill, underground, like a cave. So the workroom, though cozy and warm, always had to be lit by candles.

As she worked at her loom, Mother Lyn kept her eye on her very young children, Winkie and Tip.

"No, no, Tip! Mustn't pull on the thread . . . look out, Winkie, dear—don't get too near that candle. Oh, my, it's getting harder to keep track of you two."

Winkie and Tip were two years old, born on the same day, but they weren't twins. Winkie, the girl, was the Small-Frys' daughter. But the boy, Tip, was really their nephew and Winkie's cousin.

Tip's parents had died in a mud slide just after he was born. Mother and Father Small-Fry adopted him and were raising him as if he were their own child.

To keep them out of trouble as she worked, Mother Lyn gave the children an acorn top to play with. But Winkie and Tip soon got bored with spinning the top and quietly toddled out of the workroom. Mother Lyn didn't see them go.

The two children went past their father
who was busy dyeing cloth at a big vat in
the front room. He didn't see them, either.
They went outdoors. The mudhouse was
built on a rocky ledge, and the two children
loved to stand near the edge and look down
at the Big Valley far below.

"Big Valley," said Winkie, pointing
down. Her cousin smiled. He had not yet
learned to speak though he knew and used
some words. The tiny girl walked right to
the very edge of the rocky ledge. It was a
long three-foot drop to the ground below.
Tip came up behind Winkie and bumped her
accidentally. She teetered on the edge and
started to fall.

A big black bird swooped down toward Winkie. "C-r-r-r-u-u-k!" she called. At the same time the bird's widespread wings gently brushed against Winkie and pushed her back onto the rocky ledge. The bird landed. "C-r-r-r-u-u-k!" she called again. Winkie and Tip ran to her immediately; she spread her wings around them.

Father Len heard the black bird's warning cry and came running from the mudhouse. He was just in time to see Winkie saved from falling. "Good girl, Sable!" he cried.

Sable was one of the animals that lived and worked with the Small-Frys. They had found her when she was just a chick, about the time that Winkie and Tip were born. In two years, the raven had become a full-grown bird while the children were still babies. Sable seemed to love them and acted as their baby-sitter and protector. She had taught them to run to her when she called. Many times she saved them from being hurt.

Mother Lyn came out. "What's going on?" she asked.

"Everything is all right," Father Len told her. "Sable saved Winkie from falling off the ledge. And they ran to her when she called. It's amazing! They have really learned to obey her."

"She's wonderful!" Mother Lyn exclaimed. "You know, Lenny, I think we can take the children with us on our trip this time. Sable can take care of them. And it's time they saw something of the Big Valley."

Every year Mr. and Mrs. Small-Fry made a trip down to the Big Valley to trade their fabrics. They flew down aboard Sable, who had been trained to carry passengers.

"Do you really think so?" said Father Len. "They're awfully young." He shook his head. "I don't know."

"I think they'd be *safer* with us," said Mother Lyn. "It's so hard on Grandmom and Granddad to leave the children with them." She smiled. "And, besides, I miss them on the trips . . . they're so much fun."

"Well, I'm against it!" said Grandmom Fry the next day when she heard that the Small-Frys had decided to take Winkie and Tip with them on their annual trip to the Big Valley.

"Mark my words," said Granddad Fry, shaking his finger at no one in particular. "You'll be sorry. Why, those little tads are only *two years old*! They're still babies."

The family was gathered in the living room of the Small-Frys' mudhouse. Even Auntie Mum and Uncle Sly Fry and their children—Winkie's and Tip's cousins— were there. They were against taking Winkie and Tip on the trip, too.

"You're going to an unknown place," said Uncle Sly walking back and forth on the moss rug. "*Anything* could happen."

Auntie Mum looked over the edge of her glasses at Father Len. "Len, there's never been one good reason for you and Lyn to trade with those Big Valley Tinies," she said. "We make everything we need right here on Smoke Mountain. You're just asking for trouble by going there every year."

"Oh, but there *is* a good reason," said Mother Lyn. "Lenny and I make more fabric than we can trade with our neighbors. There are all kinds of tiny people in the Big Valley who like our beautiful fabrics. We can trade with them." She waved her hand around the room. "Look at all these wonderful bottle-bottom windows we got by trading with the Tree Tinies last year. That's why we have the sunniest front room in the village."

While the arguing was going on, the tiny cousins were looking from one grown-up to another.

"But who are the Trash Tinies you want to visit this year?" said Granddad Fry. "What kind of people would live in a town dump—disgusting!"

"You're taking our grandchildren to a town dump?" cried Grandmom Fry. "Good heavens!"

"Just calm down everybody," said Father Len, holding his hands up. "Things down in the valley are not as bad as you think they are. For instance—you probably think the tinies who live in the dump are poor and maybe even dirty, right?"

"Well, aren't they?" asked Uncle Sly. "It makes sense."

"Why in the world would they live there if they're not poor?" said Granddad Fry.

"Well, they aren't poor or dirty," said Father Len.

"How do you know?" asked Auntie Mum.

"We heard from other Big Valley tiny people that they are probably the *richest* of all the tinies because of the useful things big people are always throwing away," said Father Len. "They have built a regular city under the trash—electric lights, running water . . . everything."

"Is that a fact?" said Uncle Sly.

"Nobody knows for sure because so few people have ever visited them," Father Len went on, "but that's what everybody thinks."

"Oh, that's a fine kettle of fish!" Granddad Fry raised his voice. "You're not even *sure*, but you're willing to take the little tads with you without really knowing. Suppose these tinies turn out to be desperately poor?"

"Suppose they're robbers!" cut in Auntie Mum.

"This is silly!" said Mother Lyn, looking stern. "We've been down to the Big Valley three years in a row, and all the tinies we have traded with were clean, honest, and nice. We're *going*! So stop worrying."

"Besides," said Father Len. "You all know that Sable is fearless—she loves the children as though they were hers. She won't let anything bad happen to them, believe me."

The day finally came for the Small-Frys to leave. Sable was loaded with bolts of colorful fabrics, suitcases, and supplies. Mother Lyn put Winkie and Tip into small baskets tied to the big bird's back. She fastened their seat belts. Then, she and Father Len took their places atop the big black bird.

Grandmom and Granddad Fry were there to say good-bye. So were Auntie Mum, Uncle Sly, and their children. A few tiny neighbors stood nearby watching.

"We'll be back in about two weeks," said Father Len, "with lots of wonderful things."

"Good-bye, everyone!" Mother Lyn called.

Grandmom Fry was crying quietly. "Do be careful," she said.

Her husband put his arm around her.

"They'll be all right," he said. "I think they will."

Winkie and Tip waved good-bye. Winkie yelled, "Bye-bye! Bye-bye, Grandmom!" Tip smiled.

Sable stretched her wings out when Father Len said something to her. She flapped them slowly once, then walked toward the edge of the rocky ledge. "C-r-r-u-u-k!" she called, and hopped smoothly from the ledge to the air. Down she dropped, flying easily and gathering speed.

Winkie turned in her basket to look back.

She saw the Hill Tinies waving and yelling. She waved back at them.

The great bird soared out over the Big Valley. Then, slowly gliding on flat wings with her tail wedge-shaped, she began to circle downward.

Winkie looked at everything. Below, she saw winding roads, a patchwork of fields and houses growing larger as they came closer. Above was the top of Smoke Mountain against a bright blue sky. Everything was beautiful. A quiet rush of air was the only sound.

But Tip was busy flapping his arms and pretending he was a bird. Winkie stopped looking for a moment, then laughed and copied Tip.

As they neared the ground, Father Len signaled Sable to fly toward the southwest where the town dump was. From a distance the Small-Frys could see smoke drifting upward. Father Len pointed. "That must be where the garbage is dumped and burned," he said. "Up ahead—where the trash is— that's where we're going."

Then they saw it. The place looked like a huge accident had happened there. Everything was broken, twisted, and rusted; there was furniture, parts of old cars, machines, sinks—everything in a jumbled mess, piled up helter-skelter.

"Oh, Lenny!" Mother Lyn cried. "I can't believe any tiny people live here. It's too much of a mess."

Father Len laughed. "And they say the

22

Trash Tinies are rich!" he said. "We'll see, I guess."

The big bird landed gently on an old tire. Mother Lyn climbed from Sable's back. Her husband handed Winkie and Tip down to her.

"Now we have to find the entrance to the underground city," said Father Len. He scratched his head and looked around. "I didn't think the dump would be so big. It could be *anywhere* under this mountain of junk. I'll start looking."

Mother Lyn sighed. "That could take quite awhile," she said. She began pulling supplies off the bird's back. "I'll set up camp just in case we have to stay here overnight. Sable can watch the children."

Winkie immediately found a broken dollhouse. She walked into the living room. The house was tipped to one side; furniture had slipped to one end. The child found a chair that was standing upright, leaning against the lower wall. She sat in it. Tip climbed up beside her.

"Big house," said Winkie, looking around.

Tip clapped his hands.

Sable, still carrying the bolts of fabric on her back, flew up and perched on the doll-house roof. She turned one bright eye toward the children.

By the time Father Len returned, his wife had put up their tent. She was inside with Winkie and Tip, who were taking naps. Sable stood just outside, cocking her head this way and that. Now and then she pecked at the food Mother Lyn had left her.

"I'm not sure what to do," said Father Len. "It seems impossible to find Trash City. We may have to give up and go home or try to find some other Tinies to trade with."

Mother Lyn stood up and looked at the babies. "They're asleep," she whispered. "They played hard while you were gone, and probably won't wake up for another hour." She took her husband's hand. They walked from the tent. "I'll help you," she went on. "Sable can watch the babies."

'But . . ." said Father Len.

"Come on, Lenny," said Mother Lyn. "I'm going to show you that I'm better at finding a needle in a haystack than you are!" She headed into the messiest part of the trash pile.

Shortly after Father Len and Mother Lyn Small-Fry disappeared from view, Sable heard scratching noises behind the tent. She hopped around to the back.

Three mice were struggling to get under the tent flap! They were after the babies.

"C-r-r-r-u-u-k!" Sable flapped her wings. The mice scurried away. Sable hopped back quickly to the front of the tent.

More mice! Six or seven . . . all trying to get at the children!

"Tok! Tok! Tok!" cried the raven as she rushed at the mice. This time she managed to kill five but others came out from behind the trash.

There were mice everywhere, surrounding the tent. The big bird croaked at them, flapping her wings. The mice darted here and there trying to stay away from the bird's claws and beak. They squealed loudly.

The squeals woke Winkie and Tip. They came out of the tent—but when they saw the mice, they ran back in.

Suddenly the mice stopped fighting and ran from the area. At almost the same time, a raggedy yellow cat came bounding out of nowhere and leapt upon the raven.

There was an explosion of feathers, fabric, and fur. Around and around went the trash cat and the big black bird: claws flashing and slashing in deadly combat. The cat seemed to be winning, when suddenly Sable broke away. She reeled up into the sky. The cat leapt into the air after her, clawing madly. Raven and cat disappeared behind a pile of litter.

Moments later a band of tiny soldiers climbed out of a nearby pipe. Their leader, a distinguished-looking older officer with a beard, looked at the dead mice, pieces of cat fur, and scattered scraps of fabric. "There's been a battle!" he exclaimed.

"Some of these mice are still alive, Major," said one soldier. "It must have just happened."

"I can see that, son," replied the major. He walked toward the tent. "This tent—tiny people have been here."

Winkie and Tip pushed open the tent flap and came out. Their eyes were wide with fear.

The tiny officer ran toward the children. "What in the world!" he cried. He picked them up.

Two of the soldiers came running over. "They're just babies," one said.

The other soldier drew back the tent flap and looked in. "No one here, sir," he said. "Where are their parents, I wonder?"

The major looked down at the pieces of torn fabric and the black feathers. "Must be someone's clothes," he said to himself. Then aloud, "Look sharply, men! There's still danger here. I can feel it."

Just then Sable swooped down from the sky toward them. She was screaming, "Tok! Tok! Tok!" The raven had seen the stranger pick up the children and thought they were in danger.

The soldiers quickly began shooting stones from slingshots at the raven.

"No, no!" yelled Winkie, trying to help Sable.

"Don't worry, child," said the major. "We'll protect you."

Sable landed a few feet away and, with wings outspread, rushed toward them.

"That creature must have killed the babies' parents," said the major. "Well, it's not going to get *them*."

Suddenly the trash cat leapt into view behind the raven.

"Draw your firecrackers, men!" shouted the major. "Now!"

Immediately ten of the tiny soldiers pulled large firecrackers from their belts. Another soldier lit a match. The soldiers thrust the fuses of the firecrackers into the flame, and threw them. Ten firecrackers flew through the air, exploding around the bird and the cat at the same time.

The two creatures fled.

By now—with all the noise and confusion—Winkie and Tip were screaming at the top of their lungs.

"Hush, hush, children. You're safe now," said the major. And he carried them down the large pipe, followed by the soldiers. They all disappeared underneath the trash.

A few minutes later the Small-Frys came running back. "Where's Sable?" Father Len asked. He looked inside the tent. "Winkie and Tip are gone!"

"How could that be?" said Mother Lyn. "What happened?"

"Look!" said Father Len, pointing to the dead mice, feathers, and pieces of cloth. "There's been a big fight. Those feathers came from Sable!"

"Where is she?" said Mother Lyn. "The children *must* be with her." She looked up at the sky. The big black bird was circling overhead. "Len—there she is!"

"Good," said Father Len. "They're safe." He whistled three times.

The raven flew down and landed next to them. "C-r-r-u-u-k!" she said.

"Oh, no!" said Mother Lyn. "The children are not with her."

Father Lyn reached up and touched the bird gently. "Sable—where are Winkie and Tip?" he asked.

The great bird cocked her head and looked at Father Len. "She doesn't know," he said.

"Oh, Len, that's impossible," said Mother Lyn, shaking her head. "She *must* know. She would never desert those children. Never."

Father Len ran his hand along the bird's neck. "Something large and fierce must have attacked her. See? She's bleeding."

Suddenly the bird became alarmed. She stretched her neck and looked around.

At that point Father Len saw the trash cat. It was crouched down and sneaking slowly toward them. "Look at that huge monster!" he whispered. Then without raising his voice, he said "Get up on Sable, Lyn."

"But, the children . . ."

"Later," said Father Len. "Hurry!"

The two tiny people climbed onto the raven, who took to the air immediately. At the same time the cat charged. But it was too late—the bird was out of reach.

Later that day, the Small-Frys decided a big fight had taken place near their tent. The cat or the mice had driven away the raven and carried off Winkie and Tip. The couple didn't blame Sable. They knew she had done the best she could. Her loss of feathers and long bloody scratches showed that. She had simply been outmatched in her battle with the trash cat.

They had heard the firecrackers go off. That's why they returned to the tent so quickly. But they didn't know what had caused the explosions or even if they had come from the area of the tent. They just weren't sure what had actually happened. And, worst of all, they saw no clues that might have shown the children had been rescued.

They did, however, search and search for an entrance to Trash City. They wanted to find the people under the trash. It was their hope that the Trash Tinies could give them a better idea of what might have happened to their children.

They never found the entrance. After two days of searching through every inch of the dump, they finally gave up. It was a very sad time for Mother and Father Small-Fry.

At last they climbed aboard their wounded raven and flew back to Smoke Mountain. They were absolutely sure they would never see Winkie and Tip again.

Meanwhile, deep under the dump, the soldiers and the Small-Fry children climbed out of the large pipe. They were in Trash City. The pipe was one of the secret ways into and out of the place.

As usual, many of the underground people came over to greet their returning soldiers.

The soldiers—members of the Mouse Force Brigade—were much admired by the citizens of Trash City. Without their skill and success at fighting mice there wouldn't be a city under the town dump. The place was entirely surrounded by mice. It took a well-trained army of soldiers to make sure the people were safe at all times.

Their leader, Major Nicholas Q. Little, was the most admired of all the soldiers. He knew all about how to fight mice from a lifetime study of the animals. He had invented most of the tactics that were used. The grateful citizens of the city under the dump had even erected a statute of Major Nick, as they called him, in Trash City Park.

"Look!" cried one of the citizens when he spotted the soldiers. "Major Nick has two babies."

"Where'd you get the children?" said another.

"You and your boys just left, Major Nick," remarked a third person. "How come you're back so soon?"

"We had to come back," responded Major Nick Little. "We got into a battle with a nasty bird over these youngsters. We managed to save them, but we lost their parents. And we ran out of ammunition."

"By golly—that didn't take long," said one of the people.

"That's the way it is sometimes," said Major Little. "You can do a day's work in five minutes that can change the world forever."

The soldiers formed ranks and marched toward the center of town. Major Little held Winkie and Tip on his shoulders and walked at the head of the column. The children looked dazed—as though they didn't know where they were or what they were doing.

As they marched along, word of the battle and the saved babies spread through the town. Soon the sides of the street were filled with cheering Trash Tinies.

Winkie and Tip had been scared. But now, as they were carried along, they began to respond to the crowd of cheering and smiling faces. They started waving back at the happy people. Soon, they were smiling, too, forgetting for the moment that they didn't know where their parents were.

Major Little marched the soldiers past houses made of trash and broken furniture. One family lived in a barrel, another under a table inside a chest of drawers, and still another lived in a steamer trunk. There were even four families living in a five-drawer filing cabinet.

They marched past the town's Community Youth Center. There was a bathtub full of water for swimming in the summer and skating in the winter when the water froze. There was also a broken bicycle fixed up as a Ferris wheel.

Strings of Christmas-tree bulbs were hanging everywhere. They lighted the insides of houses and the streets.

At one point the soldiers marched past the Community Kitchen. Tiny people were standing in line to pick up food. Their containers were bottle caps of various sizes.

"What's for lunch?" cried one of the soldiers near the rear of the column.

"Carrots again!" yelled a kitchen worker.

All the soldiers groaned.

"That's three times this week!" shouted the soldier. "We'll turn *orange*!"

"Is everybody happy?" yelled the major. "Sound off!"

"*Yes!*" yelled all the soldiers. Then, "One, two, three, four!" in time with their marching feet.

When the soldiers arrived at the center of town, Major Little called out: "Column, *Halt*!"

The soldiers came to a stop. They were in front of Mayor Clutter's orange-crate house.

The mayor himself stood in front of the house. He had a bushy red beard and a black patch over one eye. And, like most of the people of Trash City, the mayor wore clothes that were spotted with colorful patches. Trash Tinies wore patches on their clothes because they *wanted* to. It was the style.

"Who are the young'uns, Major Nick?" asked the mayor.

"Two lovely children that need our help," said Major Little. "The girl says her name is Winkie and the boy is Tip. She doesn't seem to be able to tell us much more." He handed the children to a soldier. Then he drew Mayor Clutter aside to talk where Winkie and Tip couldn't hear them.

The major explained where he had found the children and said he thought their parents had been killed by a big bird.

"That's too bad," said Mayor Clutter. He sighed. "This is why other tiny people in the Big Valley seldom come to visit us. It's just too dangerous trying to find Trash City unless you know the secret ways to get here."

Major Little nodded. "I suppose Winkie and Tip's parents were trying to find their way in when the big bird attacked them."

"Well, we can't give them back their parents," the mayor said, "but we can find a pleasant place for them to live right here in Trash City. It's the next best thing to a real family." He pointed to the Trash City Home for Children across the street.

"Old Lars is the best friend a homeless child could find," the mayor went on, "and no matter how many kids lose their parents because of the mice wars, Lars always has room for them at the home and in his heart."

Winkie and Tip were taken to the Home for Children. From the outside, the home looked like a bunch of rusty tin cans. They were arranged in the shape of a tall building. Small cans were piled on top of larger ones.

At the very bottom was an upside-down washtub. There was a doorway cut into the side of the tub. Inside, the home was pleasant. It looked bright and cheerful. The man in charge was Mr. Lars T. Penny. Old Mr. Penny had lost *his* parents when he was young. He had dedicated his life to taking care of children who had the same problem.

Of course, Winkie and Tip were too young to understand why they couldn't go back to their parents. They kept asking to be taken to them. It was hard for the grown-ups to tell the children what they thought had happened. Instead, Mr. Penny and Major Little tried to get some facts.

Where did the children come from? If they could learn that, the children might be returned to their relatives. They never got a satisfactory answer.

What was their last name? The children didn't seem to know. "Well, then—how old are you?" Mr. Penny asked.

Winkie and Tip held up two fingers.

"Ah, they're both two," said Major Little. "Must be twins."

"How did you and your mother and father get to the town dump?" asked Mr. Penny.

"Sable," answered Winkie. "We flied."

Tip flapped his arms.

Mr. Penny looked at Major Little. He frowned. "What do you make of that?" he asked. "They flew?"

Major Little laughed. "Seems to me we'd have seen a glider or some kind of airplane if that were so," he said.

"Bird flied," said Winkie.

"He sure did, Winkie," said the major, "and he came zooming right down on us, too. Were you scared?"

Major Little didn't understand what Winkie was trying to tell him. He had never heard of anyone successfully training a bird to fly them places. Even if he had understood, he would have found such a thing hard to believe. And when Winkie went on to say the big bird was her "fren," the major couldn't believe she was actually trying to say *friend*. From what he had seen with his own eyes, he was sure the bird had attacked Winkie's family.

Major Little spent most of the day making sure Winkie and Tip were settled at the Trash City Home for Children. The tiny children were everywhere inside the building. Most were playing games. A few were curled up in overstuffed chairs, reading books. They all stopped what they were doing and came over to Major Little. They wanted to learn all about Winkie and Tip. The major told them where and how he had found the babies.

The children loved listening to Major Little tell stories of his adventures. Mostly they were stories about battles with mice, but

Winkie's and Tip's story was different. They wanted to hear it twice.

When Major Little left, he told Mr. Penny that he was very fond of the "twins" and that he would be back to visit them often.

"And," he said, "since we haven't found out what their last name is, I've decided it will be 'McDust' until we find out—if we ever do."

And so it was that two tiny children who had lived high up on Smoke Mountain came to live down under the town dump and were called the McDust twins.

Seven years passed. Winkie and Tip were nine years old. During those years the "McDust twins" adapted well to life in the children's home and Trash City. Mr. Penny was their father, big brother, nurse, friend, and teacher. He taught them to read, write, do arithmetic, and understand geography and the history of tiny people. They also learned some of the history of big people from old history books thrown away in the town dump.

Mr. Penny did even more than that for Winkie and Tip. He kept them from harm, taught them right from wrong, and schooled them in the art of good manners. "They were all things your parents would have done for you if they could," he said.

Outside the home—in Trash City itself—

Winkie and Tip made friends with and visited many different Trash Tinies. And, in all those seven years the two children never once left the city under the trash to go aboveground. No one ever did, except for the well-trained soldiers of the Mouse Force Brigade.

Major Little visited Winkie and Tip often, as he said he would; especially after a hard battle with the mice. Talking with them helped to calm him down. He was an old bachelor and had no children of his own. Winkie and Tip became his very special friends.

Occasionally the tiny major would bring his trained white mouse, Mus Mus, with him to the home. He used the big creature to track down ordinary trash mice. And, if Major Little ever traveled into mouse country alone, he always took Mus Mus with him. The white mouse could smell his way in and out of Trash City without running into the deadly mice packs. Winkie and Tip delighted in seeing Mus Mus do the tricks Major Little had taught him.

Every so often Winkie would ask the major to tell them the story of how he had found them years before. When he did, the major always ended by speaking of their narrow escape: "From the deadly talons and sharp beak of that big black bird."

In time, Winkie and Tip came to believe Major Little's version of the story. They forgot what had really happened.

It was almost Halloween during the seventh year of the children's stay in Trash City when they got some bad news. Major Little had just finished telling the twins for the umpteenth time about how he had found them. He suddenly said, "Well, kids—I won't be coming around to visit you so often anymore, I'm sorry to say."

"Why not, Major Nick?" said Winkie. "What's wrong?"

"Are you mad at us, Major Nick?" asked Tip.

The old soldier laughed. "Certainly not!" he said. "It's just that . . . well, I've decided to retire."

"Retire?" said Winkie. "What's that?"

"It means I'm not going to be a soldier in the Mouse Force Brigade anymore," Major Nick went on. "I'm getting too old for the job."

"You're not *that* old, Major Nick," said Tip. "Golly—you're terrific! You're still the greatest mouse fighter in the world."

"Thanks, Tip," said the major. He gave Tip a pat on the back. "I'm glad you think so. But I'm close to being sixty years old, and that's too old to be on active service in the mouse fighting business. Don't tell anyone, but my old bones are beginning to creak."

"I've never heard *that*!" said Tip, laughing.

"But you said you won't be able to visit us much anymore," said Winkie. "If you're retired you'll have more time to visit, so why can't you come *more* often?"

Major Little shook his head. "I'll be leaving Trash City, Winkie," he said. "I'm going back to where I lived before I came here."

"But, Major Nick, I thought you always lived here," Winkie said quietly.

"*I* didn't think that!" said Tip.

Major Little smiled. "Where do you think I came from, Tip?" he asked.

"I always thought you came from a far-away place," said Tip.

"Well, you're right about that—I do," said Major Little. "How'd you know?"

"Well, you don't exactly talk like the rest of the people in Trash City," Tip went on. "You have a kind of accent. It's a little different."

"Tip's right!" said Winkie. "I never thought about it before but there is something different about the way you talk. I guess I thought it was because you're the most important soldier."

"No, it's an accent," said Major Little. "Tip's right."

"And you don't wear patches on your clothes the way everyone else does," said Tip.

"Yes, although it's the style here in Trash

City," Major Little said. "You're right—I don't wear patches."

"So I imagined you lived in a house with big people," said Tip.

"Hold on there!" Major Little laughed. "How'd you figure that out?"

"It had to be some place where there were lots of mice that wasn't the town dump," explained Tip. "So I thought about houses."

"Well I'll be a monkey's uncle!" said Major Little.

"And I imagined you learned how to fight mice at the house you lived in, and because you got so mad at the mice, you came to Trash City to fight more of them," Tip continued, "because there were more of them here."

"That's pretty much what happened," said Major Little. "Amazing!"

"Tip has a great imagination!" said Winkie proudly. "Maybe he should be a detective."

"Well, Tip my boy," said Major Little. "Originally I was a House Tiny. And that's where I'm going to retire—to a house. After all these years in Trash City I'm going back to the same house I lived in when I was a boy. And, you're right—there were a lot of mice there back in '34. We had a terrible invasion of the beasts."

"Tell us about that," said Tip.

"I don't like to think about it. We lost our brother Tim." The tiny major swallowed hard. Tears came to his eyes. He brushed them away quickly. "Anyway, I'll be going home soon. I can hardly believe it. I may work on my autobiography. I think I'll call it, *Nick Little Battles the Savage Mice.*"

"Gee," said Winkie. She, too, was trying to hold back the tears, but one ran down her cheek. "We'll miss you a lot."

"And I'll miss you two a lot," Major Little said. He took out his handkerchief and wiped the tear from Winkie's cheek. "But I'm going to try and be brave about it. I hope you will, too."

"Aren't you *ever* coming back?" asked Tip.

"Sure I am, Tip. I'll come to visit as often as I can," said Major Little. "You two are my best friends."

"Good!" said Winkie. She managed a smile.

"I'll be faraway from you—halfway across the Big Valley," said Major Little. "But I do have an adventurous nephew, Dinky Little, who flies all over delivering the mail to tiny people. I'm sure I'll be able to hitch a ride with him now and then to see you."

In the next few days Winkie and Tip watched as Major Little prepared to leave Trash City. The people of Trash City gave him a big going-away party. All the important people in the city made speeches telling how much they owed to Major Little and how much they would miss him.

Mayor Clutter said: "Major Nick Little— you are not only a great soldier, sir, but you are a fine person and one smart cookie! We wish you Godspeed!" The mayor handed Major Little a handsome brass plaque that said: MAJOR NICK LITTLE: YOU ARE NOT ONLY A GREAT SOLDIER, BUT YOU ARE A FINE PERSON AND ONE SMART COOKIE!

At last the day came for the major to leave. All the soldiers in uniform were there. So were the old soldiers out of uniform. They lined up in front of Mayor Clutter's orange-crate house. Everyone who had ever served in the MFB with the major was there. They were ready to march the retiring soldier out of town. Major Little and his mouse, Mus Mus, took their places at the head of the columns of men and women.

"Forward march!" commanded the major.

It was Major Nick Little's last march. He held his head high and walked smartly. The sides of the street were filled with the citizens of Trash City. Their cheers were deafening.

At the end of the road—near one of the exit pipes—Major Little turned to the crowd and saluted. Then he waved his hand. "So long, everybody!" said the major.

The old soldier and his mouse walked into the pipe and slowly faded from sight.

Winkie and Tip went slowly back to the home.

Two months passed. One morning, a few days before Christmas, the Mouse-Alert automobile horn blew loudly. All the grownups in Trash City stopped what they were doing. They ran to their mouse-fighting stations, ready to fight an invasion of mice. In the meantime, the children and the old people went to a special fort surrounded by mousetraps.

In a few minutes Mayor Clutter rang a bell. It meant there had been a false alarm.

While the children were in the special fort Winkie heard some news. Relatives of Major Little were in the city. They had had breakfast with Mayor Clutter and were with him now, high above the city atop a stepladder. It was the observation platform where the mayor could see the entire city, the place

from where he gave the necessary orders to fight any invading mice.

Winkie found Tip and told him Major Little's relatives were in the city. "And I know where they are!" she said. "Follow me."

The tiny girl ran into the street with Tip at her heels. "Here they come now." She pointed up in the air to a tin-can elevator. It was coming down from the roof of the city.

The elevator came to a stop at the street level. Mayor Clutter led a man, a boy, and a girl out. The girl was leading Major Little's white mouse, Mus Mus, by a leash.

Winkie and Tip followed at a distance as Mayor Clutter and the strangers walked through the streets. The mayor pointed out interesting buildings. He introduced the visitors to some of the citizens. Finally they came to the Trash City Home for Children.

Winkie and Tip could see many eyes in the building's windows looking at the strangers. Mayor Clutter knocked on the front door. Winkie and Tip moved closer to hear better. Mr. Penny opened the door. "Howdy, Mayor," he said.

"This is Mr. Lars T. Penny," said the mayor. "He's the warm friend of all the homeless children who live in Trash City." Then he said, "Mr. Penny, I'd like you to meet some of Major Nick's kin: This is Mr. William T. Little and his children, Tom and Lucy."

Tom Little spoke. "Mayor Clutter—did you say *homeless* children? Do you mean there are children without parents in Trash City?"

"Yes, there are, Tom," said Mayor Clutter.

"It's the mice wars," said Mr. Penny. He shook his head. "We lose a few people every year."

Suddenly all the children from the home began to walk slowly toward the mayor and the Littles. They were staring at them. A few children ran over to pet Mus Mus.

"This is where Major Nick's special friends are," said Mayor Clutter.

"Do you mean *all* these children are Nick's friends?" said Mr. Little. "I'm afraid we . . ."

Mayor Clutter laughed. "The major used to come here often to see the children," he said. "As you know, he had no children of his own—but he had two very special friends here."

The mayor reached out and took the hands of the twins. "Major Nick found these two when they were babies, out in mouse country. No one knows who their parents were. The major was very fond of them. I want you to meet the McDust twins, Winkie and Tip."

Mr. Little said, "Why that old rascal! Nick never said his 'special friends' were children!" He shook Winkie's and Tip's hands. "Major Nick wants to see you two," he went on. "He was hurt in an accident with a cat. His sister is a nurse, and she's taking very good care of him. We borrowed his mouse, Mus Mus, to find you down here in this big pile of trash."

"Is Major Nick hurt real bad?" asked Winkie.

"Is he?" Tip asked.

Mr. Little put his arms around Winkie and Tip. "I'm sure bringing you home with us to visit the old soldier for Christmas will be the best thing we can do for him."

"Oh, wow!" said Tip. "I can't wait. Let's go!"

"Tip!" said Winkie. "Remember your manners."

"*Please!*" said Tip.

Tom Little laughed. "Tell Tip how we're going to get home, Dad," he said.

"We're going to fly home," said Mr. Little. "Our cousin, Dinky Little, is a pilot. He and his wife, Della, are going to pick us up."

"Do they know how to get into Trash City?" asked Winkie. "Everyone says it's hard to find."

"Cousin Dinky delivers the mail all over the Big Valley," said Lucy Little. "He knows *everything*!"

Mr. Little grinned and nodded his head. "They'll get here," he said.

"Gee, we're going to fly!" said Tip. "What's it like?"

"You'll *love* it, Tip," said Tom. "Wait till you see."

"Isn't it amazing?" said Winkie. "We've never been aboveground since we came here, and now we're going to fly!"

It was the Friday morning before Christmas. Streaks of light showed in the eastern sky above the town dump. The noisy engine of a gas-model airplane broke the silence.

Six tiny people sneaked out of the end of a large pipe. They kept low, moving from behind a broken pail to a cardboard box, looking anxiously about them.

"What's that loud noise, Della?" whispered Winkie to the young woman who was leading the group.

"That's an airplane," said Della. "It's my husband, Dinky. He's flying overhead in Henry Bigg's model airplane."

"Henry's the big kid who lives in our house," explained Tom. "Cousin Dinky borrowed his plane."

Della put a finger to her lips. "Let's keep

our voices down," she said. "We don't want any mice hearing us."

"Ugh! I hate mice!" whispered Lucy.

Della looked around the corner of the cardboard box. She pointed. "See the end of that broken ironing board over there? That's where I landed the glider before dawn this morning. We have to get over there fast so Dinky can swoop down and pick us up."

"How is he going to do *that*?" asked Tip.

Della jumped out from behind the box, walking fast. "Follow me—you'll see," she said. She looked up and waved at the plane as it passed by. "He sees us!" she said.

The plane dived down toward them. Suddenly a huge yellow cat leapt up at it.

"There's the trash cat they told us to watch for," said Mr. Little. "Run for it! He hasn't seen us yet."

The tiny people broke into a run, scrambling over the trash. Overhead, the airplane turned and climbed high into the air. Then it dived toward the cat. It zoomed in over the big cat's outstretched paws.

By this time Della Little and the others were climbing aboard the glider. There wasn't enough room in the cockpit for everyone, so Tom and Lucy lay down on the wings and held on hard.

The cat crept toward them slowly. Then it began to run.

The plane—now some distance away—gunned its engine, then raced toward the glider from the rear.

"Duck your heads!" Della yelled. She pointed to the hood of the glider in front of the cockpit. "Dinky's going to catch this pickup device with a fishhook on the end of a line."

Everyone in the cockpit ducked down to stay out of the way of the fishhook. The plane came in low toward the glider with the fishhook trailing out behind.

Winkie glanced up for a second. She saw something fall from the airplane.

"*Yeeeeeooowww!*" screeched the cat as it leapt into the air clawing at its tail.

"Bull's-eye!" shouted Della. "Dinky got him with one of his darts."

The model airplane, its engine roaring, came in over the glider. The fishhook hit the pickup device squarely in the middle. The glider was pulled down the ironing board runway and into the air.

The cat came charging up to the ironing board. It leapt frantically at the airborne glider and ran after it across the dump. But the glider was already too high for the cat to reach.

"Fantastic!" yelled Della over the roar of the engine. "We did it!"

Winkie and Tip were rushed to see Major Nick Little as soon as the glider landed on the Biggs' roof. First, they were taken through a secret shingle-door in the roof. Then they took a ride in a tin-can elevator. They went from the attic of the house to the Littles' apartment in the walls.

As soon as the children saw Major Little, they knew he was going to get better. "The Biggs' cat, Hildy, stepped on me," he explained. "It hurts all over but nothing's broken. At first I thought I was a goner, but I guess I'm going to stay alive."

"You're never going to die, Major Nick," Tip said.

"I hope you're right, Tip," said Major Little. "I was hurting so much I began to make plans for the end. That's why I wanted to see you two. But you've made me feel so much better, I'm just going to forget those plans. I want to tell everyone: It's great to be alive!"

Christmas at the Littles' was held in a dollhouse. It was under a Christmas tree in the

Biggs' living room. The dollhouse was a present for Mrs. Biggs' niece, Mary. But at two o'clock in the morning, while the Biggs were sleeping, the Littles passed gifts around and sang carols in the dollhouse.

Major Little told everyone the story of how he found Winkie and Tip. At one point he was telling about the attack of the big black bird. Winkie suddenly saw the yellow trash cat in her imagination. She gasped.

"Major Nick," she said. "Was there a cat there, too? Was it trying to get us, too?"

"By golly," said Major Little. "It's possible we did see that darn cat that day. It's still there, you know."

"We know that!" said Tip. "That cat was after us today, but we escaped in the nick of time."

Then all the Littles laughed because they knew the name of Cousin Dinky's glider was *The Nick of Time*.

"We fought with that cat many times," said Major Little. "I'm afraid we usually lost and had to run away."

After Christmas, Cousin Dinky flew Winkie and Tip back to Trash City in his glider. And because there was no engine in the craft, it was quiet and they could talk. Winkie looked down from on high. Everything seemed to catch her eye. She kept asking Cousin Dinky, "What's that?" and then, "What's that?" It was all Cousin Dinky could do to answer her questions and fly the glider at the same time.

Then the tiny girl saw a mountain. Winkie gasped, reached forward, and touched Cousin Dinky on the shoulder. "What's *that*!"

"It's Smoke Mountain," said Cousin Dinky. "It's beautiful today, isn't it? We couldn't see it last time because of the clouds."

"But . . ." said Winkie. "I think I *have* seen it."

"I doubt that, Winkie," said Cousin Dinky. "You and Tip have been living underground in Trash City for seven years. And you were just babies when you were taken there."

"Well *I've* never seen it," said Tip, "so how could you?"

As far as Winkie knew, Cousin Dinky and her "brother" were right. She couldn't actually remember seeing the mountain before. But . . . there it was, looming high above her against a bright blue sky—and it looked *familiar*!

Winkie and Tip were back in the Home for Children; they had to answer a lot of questions. Their friends treated them like heroes. None of them had ever been aboveground, on top of the dump. There was a lot they wanted to know about "up there."

One question was, "Did you see any clouds?" Tip said, "Clouds are just like you see in pictures, but they are higher up, and rounder and bigger than anything!"

"There are clouds on top of Smoke Mountain," Winkie added. "That's how high up it is. It was the most beautiful thing I saw on the trip."

Winkie couldn't stop thinking about the mountain. Later that day she told Tip, "I've seen it before! I *know* I've seen it before. But I just can't remember when."

"That's crazy!" said Tip. "How could

you? I've been everywhere you've been and I've never seen it."

Wanda, one of Winkie's best friends, said, "The two of you were outside Trash City when you were babies. Maybe you saw it then."

Tip shook his head firmly. "Naw," he said. "I'd remember it. Besides, babies don't know anything. *Everybody* knows that."

A few days later Winkie had a dream. In the dream, she and Tip were flying in the glider with the Littles. Winkie looked up at Smoke Mountain and said, "Isn't it the most beautiful thing you ever saw, Tip?"

When Winkie looked down she realized that she and Tip were no longer in the glider. Instead, they were flying on the back of a large black bird in the middle of a cloud. Ahead of them—also sitting on the bird's back—Winkie saw a man and a woman. Their backs were turned; the mist of the cloud kept Winkie from seeing who they were.

Winkie nudged Tip. "Who's that?" she whispered.

"Who's what?" replied Tip. He was looking right at them. "I don't see anything."

"Those people . . . right there," said Winkie. "Who are they?"

"You're crazy!" said Tip. "There are no people."

Then Winkie shouted at the two misty figures. "Who are you?"

She shouted again and again, "Who are you?" and each time she shouted the man and woman appeared to become smaller and smaller. Finally they disappeared completely from the back of the big black bird. At that, Winkie woke up.

The tiny girl had the exact same dream each night for three nights. Every time, the adults disappeared before she could find out who they were.

Winkie told Wanda about the dreams. ". . . and the black bird was just like the bird that Major Nick said killed our mother and

father," she said. "Only it wasn't terrible. I wasn't afraid of it at all."

The next night Winkie had a different dream. This time she and Tip were flying alone on the back of the big bird. The man and woman were nowhere to be seen. The bird flew higher and higher into the sky. It beat its strong wings and climbed toward the top of Smoke Mountain.

Suddenly the great bird's strength gave out. It began to circle slowly downward toward the Big Valley. Winkie woke up.

That dream was followed by another. This time Winkie and Tip and the bird almost made it to the top of the mountain. But a great wind arose and blew them away. And, again, the black bird's strength failed. It spun downward toward the valley. Winkie awoke crying and wondered why.

By now, most of the children in the home knew about Winkie's dreams. Some of them—especially Winkie, Wanda, and their girlfriends—talked a lot about what the dreams probably meant. Tip stood at the edge of the group listening. At one point, Wanda said, "I think it means that you and Tip are going to take a trip to Smoke Mountain someday."

Another girl, Bitsy, said, "No, no! It really means this: The man and the woman are really your parents, right? And they were killed by a big bird, right? And they're in *heaven*—that's what Smoke Mountain is, heaven. You said yourself it was the most beautiful thing you ever saw.

"Now . . ." continued Bitsy, "the big bird is trying to take you to where your parents are—in heaven! Only it isn't strong enough to get you there, right? In other words it wants to *kill* you—put you in heaven . . . but it can't."

Everyone was leaning forward listening.

"The reason it isn't strong enough to do it is . . ." Bitsy pointed up. "It's up there and you're down here."

"So?" said Tip.

"So, if you don't want to get killed and go to heaven with your parents, don't go up there again."

"That's the dumbest thing I've ever heard in my entire life!" said Tip. He began walking away. From over his shoulder he said, "Dreams don't *mean* anything! They're just *dreams*, that's all."

But for Winkie the dreams continued. The next was the worst of all. In the dream, the bird finally got Tip and her to the mountaintop. It flew toward a rock ledge. A tiny man and a tiny woman stood on the ledge. Winkie saw they were yelling at them, beckoning them to land. But she heard nothing. Just as the bird was about to land, a huge yellow cat leapt upon the man and woman, swallowing them. Then it turned upon the bird and struck it with a paw. The great bird tumbled from the sky toward the Big Valley with Winkie and Tip holding on for their lives.

Winkie woke up screaming.

The next night she had the same dream all over again. More children joined the group talking about Winkie's dreams. Even Tip stayed around to listen.

"I was really scared," said Winkie. "It was *so* real! I'm afraid to go to sleep tonight."

"You had a nightmare," announced Wanda. "They're terrible."

Bitsy turned to Winkie. "If you know what to do, you can change the dream," she said.

"How?" asked Winkie.

"If you *know* you're dreaming, you can stop the cat the next time," Bitsy said.

"What do you mean?"

"If you know you're in a dream, just yell at the cat, 'You're only a dream—go away!' " said Bitsy. "Then the cat will go away, and you can find out who those people are, right?"

"Wrong!" said Tip. "No one can stop a dream."

"Oh, yes you can!" said a girl, stepping forward from the crowd around Winkie. "If I'm in the middle of a dream I don't like, I close my eyes tightly and say, 'Take me to another dream,' and then I fall out of that dream and into the middle of another."

That night Winkie found herself dreaming the same dream again, but this time it was changed a little. When the bird flew toward the rock ledge, Winkie didn't see the man and woman. The cat was there, snarling and spitting. It struck at the bird with its claws.

"Get out of the way!" yelled Winkie.

Then the cat seemed to speak although its mouth never opened. "You go away or I'll eat you up for sure."

Suddenly, somehow, Winkie realized she was dreaming. She became determined. "It's *my* dream," she shouted, closing her eyes tightly, "and I command you to *leave!*"

The cat fell to the ground. The tiny man and tiny woman climbed out of its open mouth and stood up.

Now Winkie could see them clearly in the bright sunlight. As the great bird landed, Winkie leapt from its back shouting, "Mother! Father!" and ran to them.

The tiny girl woke up from her dream crying and laughing. She never felt more wonderful in her life. Now she knew her parents were alive. She knew it for sure.

Winkie realized she would never get back to sleep that night. She walked quietly over to Tip's bed and woke him.

"Are you crazy!?" said Tip. He squinted at the window. "They haven't turned on the streetlights. It's still dark."

"I have to tell you about my dream," said Winkie, "so wake up and listen."

Tip protested at first but he finally listened.

When Winkie was through, she said, "Now—I need *your* help. I've done all I can do, and I still don't know everything that happened."

"I don't know anymore than you do," said Tip. "I can't help."

"You can!" Winkie said. "You've got a great imagination. Remember that time you figured things out about Major Nick? Like he came from a faraway house and there were lots of people in his family and other things? Remember?"

"Yes," said Tip.

"You did that with your imagination—like a detective," said Winkie. "I think you can help me take all the clues and dreams and figure it all out."

Tip shook his head. "You think that black bird is friendly," he said. "Major Nick said it killed our parents and attacked *us*. I hate that bird!"

"In my dreams we fly on the bird—he's not our enemy, and the *cat* is," said Winkie. "And I trust my dreams. The dreams come from when we were two years old. We were babies, but *we were there*! We were on top of the dump when it all happened. We *saw* it."

"But babies don't—"

"And don't say babies don't know anything," said Winkie. "They do! They have brains and eyes and feelings just like we do."

Tip grinned. He nodded his head slowly. "Go on," he said.

"So I think," Winkie said, "all those things we saw when we were little came out in my dreams—only in a crazy mishmash way. But I'm sure the dreams mean the bird is our friend."

"You know something, Winkie?" said Tip. "All those dreams you told everybody—I sort of felt they were right, but I kept thinking they were silly, too. How could dreams be true?"

"Dreams are all we have to solve the mystery," said Winkie, "and a few things I think I remember . . . and Major Nick's story. And, I love him, but I think his story is wrong. I just don't think I'd be dreaming those dreams if his story were right."

"Okay," said Tip. "If your dreams are right, our family lived on Smoke Mountain, and we all flew down to Trash City on the big bird, for some reason. Maybe we were escaping something or maybe our parents heard about the place and wanted to visit it—I don't know."

"And they couldn't find an entrance," said Winkie.

"Right," said Tip. "And while they were looking they left us in the tent with the big bird on guard. Then came the mice!"

"Good!" said Winkie. Then she laughed. "I mean bad."

"The big bird killed some of the mice," Tip went on, "and the cat came when it smelled the mice, and there was a big cat and bird fight when he saw the bird instead. That's why there were feathers lying around, remember?"

Tip stopped and thought for a moment.

"I know," he said. "The cat chased after the bird, who tried to escape. . . ."

"And that's when the soldiers got there," said Winkie.

"Yeah! Yeah!" said Tip eagerly. "Major Nick didn't see them at first. All he saw was the tent and us—he said that, right?"

"So *that's* why we were all alone when he found us," Winkie said. "The cat chased after the bird . . . simple! Why didn't I think of that?"

"Then when the bird flew back," said Tip, "it saw all the soldiers around us and thought we were captured, so it attacked to save us. Major Nick thought it was after us."

"And our parents came back and found the bird all alone," said Winkie. "How sad they must have been."

"But they looked all over for us for a long time," Tip said, "and couldn't find us anywhere—so they decided the mice had got us."

"Or the cat," said Winkie. "If they saw the cat."

". . . and they flew away on the bird," said Tip. "How will we ever find them?"

"By going to Smoke Mountain!" said Winkie. "That's where they are."

That morning Winkie and Tip went to see Mr. Penny. Winkie told him about her dreams and what Tip imagined. "And so you see," she finished, "Tip and I are *sure* our parents are alive and living on Smoke Mountain. You have to help us get back to them."

But they could see right away from the look on Mr. Penny's face that he wouldn't help them. The old man put his hands on the children's shoulders. "Winkie . . . Tip," he said softly, "dreams and imagination are not the way to find the truth about real things. They're not facts."

"Well . . . okay, Mr. Penny," said Winkie. She was edging toward the door. "Anyway, thanks for listening to us." She turned, grabbed Tip's hand, and pulled him from the room. "C'mon, Tip! We're going to tell Mayor Clutter. He's *got* to help us."

But the mayor didn't believe them, either. In fact, he laughed. "Excuse me for laughing, children," he said. "It's rude of me but I can't help it." Then he looked serious. "You're asking for too much. Do you realize what a lot of trouble it would be to get you up to Smoke Mountain?"

"I know," said Winkie, "but . . ."

"It's a *big* mountain, you know," the mayor went on, "and even if your parents were up there somewhere, we would hardly be able to find them." He shrugged his shoulders. "We are tiny people, after all—and that mountain is so big."

Winkie and Tip were silent.

"I wish I could help," said Mayor Clutter. "But when all your evidence comes from dreams and imagination, well—I can't take that seriously."

But all the children in the home were convinced that the McDust twins had figured out the real story—that their parents were still alive and living on Smoke Mountain.

"Write to Major Nick and tell him,"

Wanda suggested to Winkie. "He'll help you, won't he?"

"A letter won't work," said Winkie, shaking her head, "but if I could *talk* to him, he might help us."

"He would!" said Tip. "He's terrific!"

"I don't think Mayor Clutter and Mr. Penny will take us to the Littles," said Winkie. "We have to get there by ourselves."

"You can't do that!" Wanda exclaimed. "You're only kids. You'll get lost."

Bitsy, who was listening, said, "The mice might eat them, right?" She made a face.

Tip turned to Winkie. "How are we going to get to the Littles?" he said. "We don't know the way. We flew there."

"We don't have to know," said Winkie. "We'll hitch a ride on a garbage truck. Do you remember? That's the way the Littles came here. They said it was truck number three, and it picks up garbage at their house on Friday. All we have to do is get to the dump where they park the trucks real early tomorrow morning. We can hide on the garbage truck before it gets started."

"Winkie, that's a great idea!" said Tip.

"I know," said Winkie. "I always have good ideas."

"There's just one problem," Bitsy said. "How are you going to get to the truck parking lot? The mice will probably catch you."

"We'll have to take a chance that they won't," said Tip.

Bitsy grinned. "No, you won't," she said. "You can use Major Nick's mouse to sneak past the mice. He's still here."

"Golly! Use Mus Mus," said Winkie. "Why didn't I think of that?"

"Because *I'm* the one with the good ideas!" said Bitsy.

"It *is* a very good idea, Bitsy," said Winkie. "We can borrow him in the middle of the night."

"And all of us will go with you to where the truck is," said Bitsy, "and then bring Mus Mus back before Mayor Clutter knows he's gone."

"Great!" "Terrific!" "Hooray!" shouted the children.

"Then it's all set," said Winkie. "We'll go tonight."

Early Friday morning the children sneaked out of Trash City. And, with the help of Mus Mus, they made it to the truck parking lot without trouble.

Tip and Winkie said good-bye to their friends and got aboard garbage truck number three. They hid under the seat of the cab. It was just where the Littles had hidden themselves when they had come to Trash City.

At 5:30 a man came aboard and drove the truck off to begin his rounds of picking up trash. He arrived at the Bigg family's house around noon.

Winkie and Tip jumped out of the truck's cab while the driver was picking up the Biggs' trash. They hid behind a telephone pole so he wouldn't see them. When he drove away, the two children ran across the yard to the house. They searched for and found the secret entrance that they had learned about during their Christmas visit.

The two children got aboard the tin-can elevator. They rode from the cellar to the Littles' apartment in the walls of the house. Winkie knocked on the kitchen door.

Tom Little opened the door.

"Hello, Tom," said Winkie. "We came to talk to Major Nick about something very important."

The Littles were about to have lunch. Some of them were already in the kitchen. "Who is it, Tom?" Mr. Little called.

"It's the McDust twins!" said Tom.

By this time, Lucy Little was standing alongside her brother. "It is!" she said, opening the door wide for everyone to see.

Mr. Little rushed to greet the twins. "Welcome, Winkie and Tip!" he said as he put his arms around the two children and hugged them. He looked into the wall passageway. "Surely you're not alone, are you?" he said.

"Yes, sir—we are," said Winkie.

At that point Major Little came running into the kitchen. "Winkie . . . Tip!" he shouted. "What are you doing here? Did I hear you say you came alone?"

"We have to talk to you, Major Nick," said Winkie. "It's about our parents."

"We know where they are," said Tip, "and no one in Trash City will help us find them."

Major Little took Winkie and Tip into the living room. He closed the door while the rest of the Littles ate lunch. The major wanted to be alone with the children and hear their story.

When they were finished, Major Nick shook his head slowly. "I can't help you," he said. "I'm sorry."

Tears welled up in Winkie's eyes. "Why not, Major Nick?" she asked.

"You *have* to help us!" said Tip. "You're our best friend."

"I can't help you because I just don't think it's possible to find out who and where your parents are from Winkie's dreams and Tip's imagination," said the major. "I know you two kids mean well, and I wish I could help you, I really do—but I can't."

Tip hung his head. "If you were a kid like us, you'd believe," he said.

But no matter what Winkie and Tip said, Major Nick wouldn't change his mind. He also told them they had been wrong to run-away to see him. He told them that Cousin Dinky and his wife, Della, would fly by that afternoon with the mail. Cousin Dinky, he said, would fly them back to Trash City right away. He knew Mr. Penny and Mayor Clutter would be terribly worried about them.

Winkie and Tip had lunch at the Littles. Everyone tried to be nice to them while they waited for Cousin Dinky and Della. Tom and Lucy wanted to talk about their problem with them. Major Little thought it wasn't a good idea.

It was a sad time for the children. They were so sure their parents were somewhere on Smoke Mountain. But now—without any adults to help them—they knew they could never get to the mountain to find out.

Finally it was time to go up on the roof to wait for Cousin Dinky and Della to fly in. Major Little, Tom, Lucy, and the McDust twins went up to watch them land.

The wind was blowing from the east. "That's a good sign," said Major Nick. "They'll be here soon for sure."

"There they are now!" yelled Lucy. She stood near the chimney and pointed to the eastern sky.

Everyone turned to look.

A blue-and-white glider came sailing down toward the Biggs' house. As it drew near the roof, two parachutes snapped open behind it. They acted like brakes to slow the glider down.

At the same time a fish-hook anchor was dropped from the cockpit. The anchor was tied to a long piece of twine. The glider curved down to the roof. It landed perfectly, then bounced along over the rough shingles.

The fishhook caught on a shingle and pulled the glider to a sudden stop.

Tom and Lucy ran over and grabbed the wing tips. Cousin Dinky jumped out of the cockpit and tied the glider to the roof. He turned to Della who was still sitting in the aircraft. "Nice landing!" he said.

Of course, Cousin Dinky was surprised to see Winkie and Tip. Major Little told him why they had come to see him. "And so," he said, "I want you to fly them back to Trash City as quickly as you can. Mr. Penny and the mayor must be very worried."

"I'm sure they are," said Cousin Dinky. He scratched his head and smiled at Winkie and Tip. "I think I know how you feel, kids.

When I was your age I did the same kind of thing." He laughed. "I was always imagining something and then—sometimes—thinking it really happened."

"Me, too," said Della, "especially with dreams. I remember when I was really young, sometimes I couldn't tell if I dreamed something or if it really happened."

"But it's not like that!" Winkie protested.

"Golly!" said Tip. "We know when we're dreaming. We're not babies."

Then Cousin Dinky said, "The strangest thing about this is Della and I recently heard a story about tiny people who live up near the top of Smoke Mountain—Hill Tinies."

Della laughed. "And it's really quite a coincidence," she said. "We were told they fly to places on a bird."

"Of course, it's only something we heard about," Cousin Dinky continued. "The tiny people who told us the story had heard it from someone else. I can't remember who."

"But they may be our parents!" said Winkie.

"Oh, probably not, Winkie," Cousin Dinky said. "We hear lots of strange stories when we are flying around the Big Valley delivering mail. Anyway, it's hard to believe that there could be tiny people who fly on birds."

"It does sound like a neat thing," said Della, "but if it's so easy to do, how come we've never seen it? Dinky and I travel around the Big Valley all the time."

"That's exactly what I think," said Major Little. "It just doesn't make sense. It sounds like a made-up story . . . a myth . . . even a fairy tale."

"But it's a *clue*!" said Winkie. "Couldn't we talk to the people who told you about the bird? Was it a black bird? Maybe they know something else."

"I agree with Winkie," said Tom.

"So do I," said Lucy.

"Listen, you kids," said Cousin Dinky. "I've known quite a few tiny people who tried to train birds. It never worked really. The few times it looked like it might, the tiny people flew off strapped to their birds, and no one ever saw them again."

"Maybe it has to be a special kind of bird," said Tom, "that only lives on top of Smoke Mountain."

"I think we should investigate," said Lucy, "and find out if it's true that someone saw those tiny people flying on a bird."

"Dinky," said Major Little quietly. "I think we should put an end to this kind of talk. These children are going to get their hopes up again all for nothing."

"Well, I'm *never* going to stop hoping!" said Winkie.

"Neither am I!" echoed Tip.

"Let's go, McDust twins. Hop aboard the glider," said Cousin Dinky. "We might as well get this over with."

The blue-and-white glider flew southwest toward the town dump.

"Mayor Clutter and Mr. Penny are sure going to be glad to see you two kids," said Cousin Dinky, who was piloting the aircraft from the front cockpit.

No answer came from Winkie and Tip in the rear seat.

"You had quite an adventure to tell the other kids," Cousin Dinky went on.

Still no answer.

"Someday you'll realize that Major Nick is doing the right thing sending you back to Trash City," said Cousin Dinky.

Silence.

Cousin Dinky turned around in the cockpit and looked back at Winkie and Tip. "You kids really believe in that black bird, don't you?" he said.

The children nodded silently.

"Okay, okay!" said Cousin Dinky. "I'm going to do something I shouldn't, just to prove to you you're wrong."

"Do you mean . . ." said Winkie.

". . . you're going to fly us to the top of Smoke Mountain?" finished Tip.

Cousin Dinky pointed to the clouds. "You're in luck. They're perfect for some high flying," he said. "Otherwise I couldn't do it."

"Hooray for Dinky Little!" shouted Tip.

"Those clouds are like a sign from heaven," Cousin Dinky went on. "I can't resist it."

"Oh, Dinky!" said Winkie. "You're wonderful!"

"You can forget that 'wonderful' stuff," said Cousin Dinky. "When you see that your dreams are all wrong, you won't think it's so wonderful."

The tiny pilot steered *The Nick of Time* into some warm rising air. He knew it would carry them to the top of Smoke Mountain. They rode the rising current of warm air, circling . . . ever so slowly . . . going higher and higher.

Winkie and Tip looked down on the Big Valley below. The river, streams, fields, and rooftops looked toylike to them.

Then, when the glider was almost to the top of Smoke Mountain, it shuddered and nosed downward toward the valley. Winkie saw the town dump and the smoke where the garbage was burning.

"We've lost the hot air," said Cousin Dinky. He worked at the controls trying to keep the glider from falling farther.

Suddenly Cousin Dinky found another column of rising hot air. This time they rose even higher into the sky. Then he spotted a rocky ledge and an overhanging rock. It looked like the place where he'd been told that the Hill Tinies lived. Cousin Dinky flew in and landed on the ledge.

Without warning, a bobcat bounded out of a rock cave. With one swipe of its paw the glider was knocked off the ledge. The craft spiraled downward. Cousin Dinky got control of it again. There seemed to be no damage to the aircraft.

"It's just like my dreams," said Winkie. "I feel funny."

They flew along the crest of the mountain until Tip spotted another ledge. "Over there!" he called out and pointed.

Winkie gasped. "I think that looks like our home that I saw in my dreams!" she shouted.

"Get ready for bad news," said Cousin Dinky as he landed on the rocky ledge.

The glider was immediately surrounded by a crowd of tiny people. They seemed to come right out of the rocks that were scattered about. A closer look showed there were mud-colored houses tucked away among the rocks.

Cousin Dinky stood up on his cockpit seat. By this time the crowd of Hill Tinies were gathered close up to the glider. They were touching it and talking excitedly to each other. Cousin Dinky held up both hands and shouted, "Hello!"

"Hello!" some of the crowd shouted back.

Cousin Dinky turned to Winkie and Tip. "Now you'll see how wrong your dreams and imagination are," he said. Then he spoke to the crowd, "We've flown up from the Big Valley to find out if there's anyone among you who flies around on a big black bird."

A man in the crowd raised his hand.

Cousin Dinky didn't notice him. "I know it sounds crazy," he said, "but it's important for these children to learn once and for all that there are no such people."

The crowd laughed.

The glider pilot turned to Winkie and Tip. "There—you see," he said. "The whole idea of flying on a bird is so ridiculous, these people think it's funny."

"Hold on there, sir!" said the man who had raised his hand. "You've found the person you're looking for. My name is Len Small-Fry." He motioned to a woman standing beside him. "This is my wife, Lyn Small-Fry. We do some traveling on a black bird. Who are you, sir, and what do you want with us?"

For a moment Cousin Dinky was speechless. Winkie and Tip began to climb out of the glider.

But by now Cousin Dinky was laughing. He jumped down from the glider and shook

Father Len's hand. "I can't believe you actually fly on a bird. I'm amazed."

Winkie walked up to the Small-Frys. "Did you lose two children in the Big Valley town dump seven years ago?" she asked.

Father Len looked searchingly at Winkie. "Yes, we did. But . . . how did you know that?"

"You're our parents!" said Tip. "We were found in the dump seven years ago by the Trash Tinies."

"No!" said Father Len. "They're dead. You can't be. Gone for seven years now. You're mistaken. It can't be." He stood staring at Winkie and Tip, looking like a man who had the wind knocked out of him.

Tears were rolling down Mother Lyn's face. "Oh, Lenny," she cried. "Look at them! Can't you see they're our children?"

Just then the big black raven came sailing in to land on the rocky ledge.

"It's Sable!" gasped Winkie.

"How'd you know her name?" Tip asked.

"I just remembered," said Winkie. She walked slowly toward the big bird.

"C-r-r-r-u-u-k!" said the raven.

"Watch out, children!" cried Father Len. "That's her warning."

But when Winkie and Tip ran up to her, Sable spread her wings around them.

"It's true," said Father Len, hugging his wife. "Our children have returned. It's unbelievable, like a dream."

"It was all a terrible mistake," said Cousin Dinky, "and your remarkable children figured out what really happened. It wasn't the way you thought. It wasn't the way the Trash Tinies thought, either. A sad mistake. But it's all over now, thank God!"

There was great excitment among the Hill Tinies over the return of Winkie and Tip. Everybody had to shake their hands and give them welcoming hugs. After they had all calmed down, questions were answered and explanations given. At last everyone understood what had happened seven years ago at the town dump.

Winkie and Tip were taken to their home for a reunion with all their relatives. To their surprise, they were introduced to seven-year-old twin children of Mother and Father Small-Fry. And, to their further surprise, they learned they were cousins and not twins.

"It's kind of crazy, though," said Father Len. "Winkie looks like my sister, Mady, who was Tip's mother."

"I know," said Mother Lyn. "And Tip looks like you!"

"That's the way it is in families," said Granddad Fry, shaking his head and looking at Grandmom Fry.

"I know," said the old lady. "It's a wondrous thing!"

Before leaving, Cousin Dinky took everyone for a ride in his glider. As he took off to return to the Big Valley, Winkie and Tip flew a little way with him aboard the big raven.

"I'll tell everyone in Trash City what happened," Cousin Dinky called across to the children.

"Tell them we'll come to visit as soon as we can," said Winkie.

"Boy!" said Tip as he stroked the bird's sleek feathers, "I can hardly wait to take a trip back to Trash City on our wonderful big black bird."

"C-r-r-r-u-u-k!" said Sable as she wheeled in the sky over the Big Valley and headed for home.

EPILOGUE

"*T*he end," said Uncle Nick as he closed the book. "I wrote the story as I remembered it."

Tom and Lucy clapped their hands.

"Not so loud, children," whispered Mrs. Little. "Baby Betsy is sound asleep. I'm sure she was listening. Babies *do* know more than we think."

"And, of course, I did tell Mr. Penny and Mayor Clutter that Winkie and Tip found their parents," said Cousin Dinky. "They were very surprised. But the children in the home weren't. They said they knew it all along."

"Well, *I* was astounded!" said Uncle Nick.

"You mean because the big bird was flying the Small-Frys around the Big Valley?" asked Mr. Little.

"No," said Uncle Nick. "Because I didn't think our dreams and imagination could solve problems, when they most certainly can."

"Amen," said Mr. Little, "and *amen*!"